Goodnight Little Village

Briana McGee

About the Author

Briana McGee is a 12 year old girl who has the mind of an English teacher. Since I was young, I have loved to write. I would always write random stories whenever I could. This book is one that I wrote when I was 9, but then revised and worked with it 3 years later. Not only do I do well in school and write, but my family has a dairy farm, and I have my own beautiful show cow named Pepper, and she's my whole world. I hope to publish more stories.

Once upon a time there was a little village with lots of sleepy people.

They said to the village every night, "Good Night Little Village."

They dreamed of glittering
houses and shining moonlight.

Then, when the people went to bed, all of their dreams were magical.

One little girl named Grace, had
a dream that at night the
village was different in the
moonlight.

It was shinier and glitterier. Something Grace would love very much if she could see while she's awake.

But everyone in the village had
to sleep for it to happen
because they could only see it in
their dreams.

Then one night when Grace
went to sleep, she saw what she
thought was glitter outside, but
she was too tired to look.

Grace

While Grace was sleeping, she woke up to someone calling her name.

Follow
Me
outside.

She saw a little fairy on her pillow. The fairy told Grace to follow her outside.

Once Grace had made it outside, she saw that the buildings and the sky were all glittery and magical just like in her dreams.

She didn't know what was
happening, so she asked the
fairy, "Why can I see the world
like in my dreams, but I am
awake?"

The fairy told her "I want
everybody to enjoy the world
when it's magical all the time!"

So now every night even when people are awake, they can see outside all glittery and magical just like in their dreams.

GOODNIGHT
LITTLE VILLAGE!

Good night little village!

www.ingramcontent.com/pod-product-compliance
Lightning Source LLC
Chambersburg PA
CBHW061146160726
48006CB00038B/2295